THE UN FINISHED LOVE SONG

AF434806

CHANDRA KUMAR

Copyright © CHANDRA KUMAR
All Rights Reserved.

This book has been self-published with all reasonable efforts taken to make the material error-free by the author. No part of this book shall be used, reproduced in any manner whatsoever without written permission from the author, except in the case of brief quotations embodied in critical articles and reviews.

The Author of this book is solely responsible and liable for its content including but not limited to the views, representations, descriptions, statements, information, opinions and references ["Content"]. The Content of this book shall not constitute or be construed or deemed to reflect the opinion or expression of the Publisher or Editor. Neither the Publisher nor Editor endorse or approve the Content of this book or guarantee the reliability, accuracy or completeness of the Content published herein and do not make any representations or warranties of any kind, express or implied, including but not limited to the implied warranties of merchantability, fitness for a particular purpose. The Publisher and Editor shall not be liable whatsoever for any errors, omissions, whether such errors or omissions result from negligence, accident, or any other cause or claims for loss or damages of any kind, including without limitation, indirect or consequential loss or damage arising out of use, inability to use, or about the reliability, accuracy or sufficiency of the information contained in this book.

Made with ♥ on the Notion Press Platform
www.notionpress.com

Dedicated to the silent romantics, whose hearts brim with unspoken emotions and whose journeys are etched with the enduring imprint of a love unvoiced. For those who carry the torch of unexpressed affection.

Contents

Foreword

The characters and events portrayed in this book are fictitious. Any similarity to real persons, living or dead, is coincidental and not intended by the author.
No part of this book may be reproduced, or stored in a retrieval system, or transmitted in any form or by any means, electronic, mechanical, photocopying, recording, or otherwise, without express written permission of the publisher.
ISBN: 978-93-6128-671-1
Cover design by: Notion Press

Preface

In the pages that follow, embark on a journey through the intricacies of a poignant love story. As the chapters unfold, you'll witness the serendipitous meeting of a young boy and girl during their college days—a tale woven with the threads of unspoken emotions and missed chances. Life takes them on separate paths after college, only to reunite in the tapestry of their careers. The echoes of a love that couldn't find its voice resonate through time. Join the characters on a poignant exploration of love, loss, and the enduring power of memories.

Acknowledgements

Hi all,

It cannot possible to thank every one who has contributed and encouraged me to write this book.

Every character persent in this book are some where inspried me and loved me since my college days and continuing it till present day. I really wanted to thanks for all of them.

The one I would like to thanks here are

To my Parents, for giving me this much.

To My sister who stays with me in every time and encourage me to route this path.My college friendswho were there with me in every part my college days and till today and my lovely three idiots gang.

To the all me dear collegues who helped me start is path and still encoraging.

And finally to the character Amrutha.

Prologue

In the pages that follow, embark on a journey through the intricacies of a poignant love story. As the chapters unfold, you'll witness the serendipitous meeting of a young boy and girl during their college days—a tale woven with the threads of unspoken emotions and missed chances. Life takes them on separate paths after college, only to reunite in the tapestry of their careers. The echoes of a love that couldn't find its voice resonate through time. Join the characters on a poignant exploration of love, loss, and the enduring power of memories.

1
Dream Come True

28th June 2022, the time is almost 4:30 in the evening, everyone is busy with work,

meanwhile my phone rang.

'*Hello CK, what time will you come?*' A lady's voice asked on the phone.

'*5 o'clock*' I said

'*Ok fine*'

'*When you started, call me*' she said

'*ok*' I said and hung up.

Meanwhile from behind, I heard the call "*what Chandra leaving early?*" asked Ram Niwas.

He is Six years older than me. I am a junior there. He never showed me seniority. Very friendly with all those who go together.

I asked, "*You are not leaving?*"

He said '*I am already packed up man, ready to go*'

'*I am also leaving, urgent work to do*' I said

Then Kiran said from the side that '*he is going to meet his girlfriend*'

'*No man, he doesn't have that much talent*' said Nilotpal.

But I was smiling as if I had heard their words and I was preparing everything to log off.

I started by saying '*ok bye team bye, bye to everyone*'

But Kiran shouted that '*good luck man all the best*'

I thought how did he know hat I am going to meet a person? I had given a dangerous look to Kiran but he ignored it and said all the best.

When I reached the lift lobby, there was already a group of people waiting for the lift. Meanwhile, my phone rang again and I picked it up and answered it,

'*Have you started?*' she asked in the phone

'*I will be there in an hour*' I said and cut the call.

Almost 5 minutes have passed while waiting for the lift but still it is playing a lift game based on first come first serve.

So, I took the stairs not because of myself. Our office is on the ninth floor. As each floor goes down, I feel more and more anxious. For some reason, I am going to meet the person whome I wanted to meet for 3 years. I am anxious and happy.

As I was going down each floor, many questions started pouring in my mind, how is she doing, what should I talk to her, so many small questions started in my mind.

Strangely, I am more reluctant to talk. If it is a new person then I am silent, but if they ask anything, all one-word answers that's the problem. Yes, it is! Because of this problem, I thought a little bit about talking to her, but these little questions were born from that problem.

After a 10 mintes walk I reached bus stop. Buses were keep coming but there is no place to sit in even a single bus. As it is evening, everyone has just left for their homes, so none of the buses are empty.

So I booked a cab online as it is not appropriate to wait for the bus. Anyway, the booked cab came in five minutes, said OTP and sat relaxed in the back seat.

However, the mind is never free, always thinking about something. As long as we are in the office about work, when we go to lunch about food, salary, financial problems, we keep thinking about something like this.

While relaxing in the back seat, I remembered what we had discussed last time when I met her, Three years back engineering final year, last before Semester and last day. We both had lunch together and wished each other well. Then she left and I was looking at her.

ᗅᗅᗅ

So, while remembering the moments of my last time meeting with her, my destination arrived. Meanwhile the auto driver said that your stop has arrived so, I come back to the present day.

I paid him money and opened my mobile and called her.

I got the answer that she is coming in two minutes and the phone hung up before I could say anything.

That moment is still in my mind. The place is surrounded by green trees and lily flowers falling from the trees here and there on the road giving a new romantic feel. I don't know the names of those trees and the names of the flowers, but they are yellow and red in colour and they are lying on the foot path and road.

If any vehicle passes on that road, the flowers rise up to the force and create a romantic atmosphere. In addition to that, songs are coming on the radio from the small shop next to the road.

So, I was waiting in the sitting area which is opposite to her hotel. In exactly two minutes I saw a girl coming out of the main door of the hotel. Suddenly a car went fast on the road and immediately I took two steps back. The yellow and red colour flowers on the road flew in the wind towards the force where the car went. The force of the wind caused her hair to open like a rose. In the middle, her face, her smile, as if she had given love to a Mani Ratnam movie, that moment remained in my mind.

'Hello CK how are you?' She came near to me and asked.

'Hay Amrutha!'

'I am good, How Are You?'

'It's been 3 years waiting for this moment. Finally, it's good to see you in Bangalore.'

'And welcome to Bangalore miss Amrutha.'

She gave a little smile saying don't overreact.

"No Miss My Dream Comes true."

"I have a wish that always wanted you to come to Bangalore."

"Thank God my heart has been fulfilled for so many days." I didn't gave chance to her talk

'Hoo you are the culprit that I want to come to Bangalore. because of you again now I have to take care of everything like room and facilities' she said with a smile.

I said OK, let's talk somewhere while drinking coffee.

Ha no coffee, there is domino's nearby. Can we eat something and talk? I am very hungry.

We both said OK and started walking together.

The restaurant is near us, just a 2-minute walk. We both went to the restaurant together,

I ordered 2 pizzas and while I was paying the bill, she stopped me and she only paid.

Boys should be lucky if the girl pays the bill. I got that luck today.

We both went and sat and she started talking.

All good everything is going well now because of your curse I am in Bangalore. New City, New People, New Language and First Most New Job. Let us hope all things will turn out well.

Oddly, she is very talented and she is always first in academics. Whenever I talked to her, I never mentioned anything personal, except mostly things about academics Not only with me, she is very friendly with anyone and talks very comfortably.

we do generally behave like that, when we want to do and say instantly. If there is in and out in out thoughts it is not possible.

yes, it's right I have a kind of love for her. I like her words, her behaviour, her simplicity, her courtesy to others and the love she shows to her loved ones.

I loved her since my college days and still loving her because, what more than this a boy needs to love.

She doesn't know about this. nobody knows about this except my diary. It's So Strange by Keeping the Secret from the Past Seven Years.

I never tried to say this because every time I got the thought, I was afraid that if I told her, she would agree or not, if she would stop talking,

so every time I got the thought, I kept postponing the attempt. Moreover, both of us are in the same college and we always plays jokes on each other so that's why I don't like to disturb that atmosphere by talking about my love and that's why I always call her Amritha ji because She is Amrutha and she also always makes fun of me by calling CK.

So, that day we had a fun talk at the restaurant and shared things with each other.

We talked about the present job and meanwhile the pizza arrived and we both started eating together.

She asked *"what else CK has a good job, education is over, when will you get married ?"*

Suddenly I was shocked that she asked such a question and now I am feeling a little that, what should I answer.

She noticed it and said *"Hey I asked casually if you don't want to say then don't say."*

"No, no, I have a sister. We are watching matches for her maybe after her marriage mine would be." Said and relaxed at that moment.

I don't know why, when I have to talk about such topics with her, I feel uncomfortable. Maybe it's because I love her but I like that feeling very much.

So, let's divert the topic somehow and talk about new technologies and other job matters.

It's already two hours and you will be late, let's go, she said.

I reluctantly said OK.

We both taken a selfie and I gave her company till the hotel and said one word before leaving.

Thanks for making my day beautiful. I have been waiting for this moment from the day we met.

It's ok CK I will be staying in Bangalore from now on. We will catch up whenever we have time, she smiled and went inside the hotel.

I took a cab to go to my room. From the location where I'm right now to my room, it takes a minimum of one and a half hours, which is 7 at night. Bengaluru city is famous for its traffic as much as it is famous for IT industry or silicon city.

So much so that the software engineers working here go to their office daily for two hours and finding delivery apps to deliver items within 10 minutes. The sad thing is that I am one of them. What can we as common people do, except that I am one of the lakhs of people who were born somewhere far away from the village and abandoned by the parents and came to Bengaluru for a job.

So, the cab started, the traffic was a little heavier than usual, so the driver was going a little slowly, and I was sitting in the back seat, remembering everything that had happened today. And so, my thoughts went from the moments to when we first met to the days after.

Anything that works fast in this world is our mind. It will go where ever it wants, to our past and moments and memories.

"The memories of the story are sometimes happy and sometimes painful. Good or bad memories stay with us till the end of us.

❦❦❦

"

2
The day I met her

June 12, 2016 was my first day of college. Actually, I am CHINA batch student.

Do you mistakenly think that I studied in China? Not at all. CHINA means Chaitanya Narayana's batch.

In fact, these 2 years of my intermediate are horrible to imagine After my SSLC and the 2 years gap between the first day of college, I forgot that I am a human being and became a robot fighting only for marks.

Don't know the day or week or either year only study. It starts at five in the morning, the race will end at 11:00 at night, but there will be a two-hour break in between for lunch. After doing that hard work, as a result, I got a good rank in the EAMCET exam and also got a free seat in SV College, Tirupathi. That's how I started college.

Actually, BTech and more on computer science in it, I don't worry about marks because those 2 years vibe is still there. That's all, once a batsman gets into form, runs and marks come in like a flood.

But the problems that came were my introverted behaviour, new place, new people, there were one or two people who knew me, but they were seniors than me, so I felt a little uncomfortable.

Well, whatever happened, I went to college early in the morning. When I was going, everyone had come and sat inside. Just then another boy who came with me followed me and sat next to me and started talking for a couple of minutes. Because I wouldn't do it anyway.

Hi my name is Naveen

Hey hi, my name is Chandra Kumar

After saying that, the next question is *'what is your rank in the EAMCET ?'*.

I felt bored as he was talking about marks and ranks.

I said "*Mine is 7000 bro*"

He said "*Ho mine is 6000*"

He asked again "*Which college are you in?*"

I said "*Chaitanya Vijayawada*"

he said "*Mine is also same bro Chaitanya Vijayawada*"

So, we both talked for a while and in those words we both learned that we studied at the same place.

We became friends for a while. While talking like that, the staff came to explain the formalities.

Admission staff were gradually checking whether everyone had come, my turn came, I told my details and looked back.

That's the first time seeing her. Long hair white chudidar with pink dupatta, bright eyes and with sweet voice said excuse me as if to give way to her At that moment

I forgot that I was in the class. I kept looking at herself until she left and that was the first moment I saw her, but that moment still remains in my mind.

So, the admission process was over and some friends were made. So, the first day in college is complete and the high light of the whole day is seeing Amrutha

But un fortunate thing is I joined in CS department and she joined in IT department That's how the first week of my college days went by. New admissions were coming, getting to know each other more and more about their friends, and what's more, the main subject courses hadn't started yet.

Regular classes started from next week, I was looking at her daily in the campus but didn't dare to speak, then BRUNT THE BRAIN course has started for the first year.

BRUNT THE BRAIN is a computerized programming session where people who were passinate about the programming and problem solving were joined. even I too joined. Basially here they provide a real world problem and our job is to find out the degital solutions for those problems.

To tell you the truth, I didn't even know what a computer was until I went into the conference room. I never saw it directly except in a movie.

That's why I didn't even have a mobile until then. All we knew was only book knowledge. Now there are laptops, iPods, compact desktop, but in college they have Windows 7 and still using CPUs with large desktops

I will never forget the first programming session in my life I accidentally went to the room 10 minutes late. How I became a software engineer makes me laugh now, but back then I didn't even know how to turn on a computer.

I looked around to see if everyone was in my situation and everyone was opening something and typing and there was a sound of tuk tuk, then I felt that this is not a place that would suit me.

Well, if we don't know, the first thing we see is our neighbours Lochan is there, I spoke once or twice a week ago Well, I tried to ask him, but he is already talking to Sri.

Looking back at this, it's Amrutha, I felt very happy for a moment. But I was afraid to talk to her, so I looked at her for a couple of minutes while I was getting lost in myself.

But she didn't look at me and I'm looking if she would give me eye contact.

She turned to me and said hi when she noticed that I was looking at her.

I said '*hello*'

She was typing something and I plucked up the courage to ask '*what are you all doing?*'.

She said that she is revising the programming concept that she know.

First time I hear the word programming.

Well, I don't know what to do, so I asked her if she could explain a little.

She took my system and opened the editor and wrote a small C program.

If the readers were software engineers, please don't laugh, she wrote an addition of two number program in C language.

She was typing something, I didn't understand. I was simply watching. I did not understand anything, but it was the first time I saw such things, what I know is only physics and mathematics.

But at the end she explained everything and It was the first time that I was talking to an unknown girl for so long and that feeling was very new.

Talking to her like that gave me a good feeling This programming sessions used to be held three times a week.

I specifically wait for that sessions because I can talk to her. But what is surprising is that she always talks about studies. I also always talk about the subject with her but never asked about her personal things like where her hometown, hobbits are? I don't know why but she doesn't even give me space to ask such things.

And the second thing is that almost the first semester is over, I have made many friends. She has many friends. But she never spoke outside the lab except in the sessions, and if I dares to speak in the canteen or in the campus, she always has two bodyguards around her I don't remember the name of one of them, one is Devi for sure.if any boy talks to her, they will kill them with just a glance.

ᗞᗞᗞ

3

The Dream

So the first semester holidays came I used to go from Tirupati to Bangalore because at that time my parents were staying in Bangalore so mostly I prefer night journey,

if I start at night 11 PM I would reach Bangalore by morning five.

But it is very difficult to get buses from our college to Tirupati bus stand in the evening times.

so we used to come to the bus stand a little early But like now, there were no mobiles then, so I thought let's pass the time, put the luggage in the locker and left to see the whole bus stand again.

Looking back, I came to Vizag bus terminal and stopped Surprise!!!

"Hey Amrutha very good evening" I said

Luckly doesn't have any bodyguards by her side so I can happily talk to her. T

hen I got a chance to talk to her and through her words I got to know her hometown is Vizag. At present we are in Bangalore but my mother's hometown is next to Vizag so I have a little idea.

I asked if she had dinner?

'Ha My dinner is over'

'Have you eaten?'

'Not yet. Now have to go and eat' I told a straight lie.

She said 'ok then go and eat'

I thought to myself that we don't know that. I asked her

'where can I find the best taste here?' I asked

then she said 'Near here there is Sarvana Bhavan. taste is good, I just ate it, you should try it once'

then I took two steps back and looked back again saying that

it's okay, I'll go and eat there

She asked 'what CK ?'

I asked 'I am alone, can I have some company for dinner?'

She said 'no CK I will miss the bus'

Then I understand that even though there is still 2 hours time for the bus to come, she says she won't come, which means she doesn't want to come

I said ' it's ok Amrutha ji, it's ok'

She smiled a little She said 'ok bye and have a happy journey'

I took two steps back and made a fun challenge

' Remember that one day I will have lunch with you and as a bonus I will take a selfie also'

She heard that and said 'all the best'

Then I sent off to her from a distance and left. She didn't notice me but I was walking around her Without having a small doubt until her bus started, her bus started and left. After some time, my Bangalore bus also started.

❦❦❦

4

Love Seeds

After semester holidays, we all came back to college,

Still never talked to her outside, only talking to her in the lab, ten days passed like that Semester results just came

.

As I am an average student so I got 83% and Naveen also got 89 I don't remember exactly.

Well, I wanted to ask what percentage for Amrutha,

somehow I got a mobile phone when I came back from holidays, so I thought I should ask someone for her number,

then I understood that At Least I would be better to talk to her in the lab but other guys have never talked to her.

Then called Sri and asked if he had her number.

He has her number but he said he didn't given,

he told me that it is not good to give another girl's number.

I didn't ask him again.

After five minutes the WhatsApp group invitation notification came.

Sri created it only for our class then I joined in it, all the numbers of my class are in that group. Amrutha's number also there in the list,

I thought thank you Sri and took the number and saved it as Ammu and started chatting.

Hi

Hay CK

She saw my WhatsApp DP and identified my number and therefore remembered it as CK

'*How are you?*' I greeted

'*I'm good . What about you?*' she replied

'*I'm good*' I replied

'*Hay did you check your results?*' I asked again

'*Haa I did, results were good enough*' she said

'*How much did you get?*' I asked

'*Guess?*' she asked

I said '*93 %?*'

she repled '*Little close It's 95%*'

After seeing that message I understood why she said no to me for dinner.

Basically girls like this are always alike.They talk very little and talk to very few people.

'*How much did you get?*' she asked me

I didn't reply again and I didn't get any message from her either.

We met again in the next BRUNT THE BRAIN session. This time I didn't say anything when she came she said '*hey good morning CK*' she greeted me

I looked at and gave a small smile and then looked at my system.

She was also looking after her work without talking again.

I was pretending to be working. Something was stirring inside and an hour passed.

She didn't speak. I didn't speak

She said *'what CK are you so busy , didn't even say hi'*

'No no, nothing like that, I was just ..'

'you are doing some work right' I said

'What happened CK?' She asked if everything is ok?

'All Fine Amrutha ji, Nothing Just...' After two minutes she spoke again

'Hey, by the way, what is your score, there is no reply to the message' she asked

Then I looked at her and gave an expression, look, same like Brahmanandam in the movie Money money more money , then I thought in my mind

Hey, did this girl ask knowingly or what else After 20 seconds,

she looked at his system and said, *'What are you looking at?'*

'I did not get the dictator's score' I answered somewhat sarcastically saying that something came according to our knowledge

'Don't do overact ,Tell me how much you got' she asked

I said '83%'

she told *'Hay nice well done yaar'*

for theat I replied *'Stop the overreaction. you are doing now'*

After a while, I started talking like I always do That day was a little fun in the session, that day I realized that she is a very mature girl ,who doesn't even care about the quantitative things.

Two years have passed so if you look at the time it has been 2 years but so far I have never spoken to her outside except in the conference room.

Whenever I tried to talks outside, bodyguards will come in between. But what makes me happy is that we talk heartily as much as we talk in the lab and I like it very much.

I would love to talk to her, I don't know the actual time when I talk to her, the day I talk to her is very exciting. But every time I went on holiday, I met her at the bus stand. I always invited her for dinner, But every time I got the same answer NO, and I was accepting it with a smile.

I don't know , but why did I like her more, the way she talks, the sarcasm is her talent, attracted me to her, I was in love with her without knowing it, but I didn't know this until many days later.

ᗠᗠᗠ

5

Last days in college

It is the final final year for us, everyone is preparing for the placements.

I am also preparing for, Of Course, I'm not the type of person who drops out of studies in the name of love. In that process, she got the job before me .

She was talented and I didn't feel anything new in that.

After a month I got a job in Infosys, of course I am also an average student.

So I messaged after the day when I got the job

'*Hay Amrutha*' I messaged '

"*Hay CK* "

"*Why did you send a message after so many days?*"

'*By the way congrats for the new job*' got the response from her

I don't think she knows anything about me but I'm wrong, she knows everything about me.

surprising thing is that she didn't talks to other people a lot except with three idiots but she knows everything.

I said '*Tq and same to you*'

she replied '*Tq so much*'

I asked '*Shall we catch up for lunch?*'

I did 100% predict that she will answer NO but surprisingly she replied

'ok this Sunday'

I thought shock, oh my god she finally accepted my invitation.

'Sure, I'll be eagerly waiting for this.' I texted back

After 2 days it's Sunday afternoon time around 11 AM I got the message from her

'When can we catch up?'

I replied 'Your wish, your comfort is mine'

'12 @F5?' she asked

'Sure' I replied back

By the time I stared at my room I got the call from her

'Hay CK, where are you?' she asked

I said 'I'm on the way , 5 min'

'Okey okey come fast' she replied I asked

'Did you reach?'

'Haa 5 mins ago' got the response

Then I told 'Ohh okay ... Coming....'

Even when I go to a restaurant, she booked a table and waits for me.

She is the same Amrutha the same grils looking from 4 years but why does she look new today?

I always see her in callege attair. but today she is in saree. When I saw her in my favorite color, she was looking very new. I went and sat in surprise.

'Hey CK, come . Why late? As a girl I came fast Why are you getting ready so late ? ' she started asking.

but I am still in surprise , I have always wanted to have lunch with her.And today it is,I'm very excited and happy.

Breaking my thoughts, she nudged me lightly with her hand and said

'What sir what is going on, be alert'

then I said '*Hey sorry sorry I'm absent*'

'*Tell me what to order CK ?*' she asked

'*What do you like?*' I asked

'*I don't have anything specific, any rice item is ok*' she said

"*Biryani?*" I asked

Haa okey, biryani with coke

Called the waiter and ordered. after she started talking

'*What CK got the job, what next?*' she asked

'*Leave me aside, what about you?*' I asked

she said '*Mine is all normal ,My sister is older than me. She has completed her B.Tech CSC in JNTU and she is already working. Her marriage may be this year or next year. After that there will be a gap of three four years and after that my marriage will happen, I already know everything that will happen in my life.*'

'*Who will plan life like this, like a house plan, you are a practical person to look at.*' I asked

'*Of Course I'm*' she replied the I said

'*So there are two software engineers in the house*'

'*Yes ..*' with a smile from her

'*How many Siblings do you have?*' she asked

'*I have a sister who is two years younger than me. This job is for her. For now, father and I have to plan things for her marriage*' I replied

'*Great, very nice!!!*'

'When is your marriage?' she asked

'How can you get married after your elder sister, same way I too will think about myself after my younger sister, there is still a lot of time for that' I replied

'Are there any other goals?' she asked

'Yes, for now, I have to earn money and help my family at home. Later, if possible, I should try for higher education by all means' I said she said 'Nice, very good!!!'

'*What! don't you have?*' I asked again

'*I don't have much, I have to do some job, I have to live my life peacefully, then somehow I will get married, I want a simple family life*' she replied

I can't expect this answer from her, her talent, her behavior has nothing to do with this answer.

'*So you got a job, even if it's a little late, the next step is marriage?*' I asked

'*That's it for now*' she replied

'*Like any love ?*' I asked with slow voice

"*I don't understand what is it?*" she asked

'*Nothing*'

'*Don't be shy, I won't feel anything please be free*' she asked again

then took some breath and asked again

'*Anything like love?*'

the she replied '*No Chance At present there is nothing like that .total permission on parents*'

After hearing that word, increased respect on her then I asked

'*At Least like or crush on anyone?*'

'*Hay no CK nothing like that*' she replied instantly

still I asked more interestingly '*Hey come on , don't lie , at least must have a crush on someone, tell me I won't tell anyone*'

'*True CK, nothing like that*'

' *my work in college and again my room that's it*' she replied

what she would think if I ask more about So, that's why I ended the topic .

'*Do you have anything like love that's why you are asking so much?*' she asked

I was really stumped by that question

'*It is the only thing less for my life that I don't have that much of a scene*' I said

but she said '*Anyone can like your CK , you are a good person*'

I don't know why I felt a little happy satisfaction in my mind by hearing that from her.

While we were talking, our order arrived, we both started eating and we talked a little about our career, talked about new technologies.

three hours of eating and talking passed without realizing it. While talking like that, I heard the sound of my phone and I saw that the mail came in. I urgently opened the mail and saw it After reading the mail for two minutes

'*hey got it man*' I shouted with joy

'*What happened CK*' she asked me

then I said '*Hey, I got a three month internship offer, mail saying that I will be in Mysore for 3 months in the last SEM , and have to join in the next week.*'

I don't know why the next second was full of dullness because now it's time to tell the bye to Amrutha.

Maybe this is our last meeting.because I have to prepare everything to go to Mysore like a passport etc. So I have to go to the village for 2 days, It hurts a lot

'*Congrats CK, all the best*'

'*Yeah yeah ... Thanks you*' me with low voice

she asekd '*Shall we go?*'

'*Yeah. yeah* ' came from me Unknowingly

I was about to ask my situation to get up again and pay the bill, but she pushed me aside and paid the bill without listening to me.

Coming out of the restaurant, I felt very heavy but I don't know why. There is a disturbance inside as if something is going at a jet speed and it is an unknown pain.

"Ok CK we will meet again " she said and left towards the hostel and I kept looking at her.

Without knowing it, my eyes got wet that day.I kept looking at her until she disappeared, but that moment was very painful.

I didn't feel that much sad when she said NO to my invites. But I felt very sad when she left.Something wanted seemed to be slipping away.

After she left, I cleaned myself, wiped my eyes, took out my phone again, called my parents and told them about my first job and internship and they were very happy.

Ever since she left, there was some unknown anxiety, I didn't even want to eat dinner in the evening. My body temperature dropped a lot, I couldn't sleep, I was thinking all night, and the next day when I saw her in college, my heart beat increased a lot.

It was a little difficult so I came to the room in the middle of the college and said let's go home, I grabbed my luggage and left for Bangalore. Whenever I went to the bus stand, She used to meet me at the bus stand but this time it was not like that and it still hurt.

After three days I got ready to go to Mysore and came to college along with some other people coming from Mysore internship so they all planned to go to the night bus together. Ok, let's message Ammu once

' *ji ,Shall I call you?*' I texted her

After a few minutes she answered

'*No CK I'm a bit busy and went home and will call you when I'm free again*' .

then I message '*Tonight I'm leaving tirupati.I have a joining date tomorrow.*'

'*Great CK Wish you all the best*' got the reply from her

I said '*Thanks you,Miss you Bye*'

Got the couple of smile emojis as a reply.

After reaching Mysore, everything is set, room ,climate, food is fine, everything is going smoothly, morning workout, after training, after internship project, after dinner, that's it.By 9:30 in the night I used to go to bed after everything was complete but there was a gap between going to bed and falling asleep, that gap was very difficult to pass.

Every time I remember her before going to bed, Sometimes I get a thought that I should call her and talk , but if she feels annoyed, that's why weekly once I used to call her . I wanted to talk to her so many things , but she didn't give me that chance and space , every time we used to talk about the internship things and new technologies that we learnt.

After two months, the corona lockdown started and my internship was also stopped in the middle and I was sent home. She was also stopped by the college and sent home. After that the college did not start and the rest of the college things were done online.

At least I wanted to meet and talk to her for the last time. Unfortunately, Corona didn't give me that chance. Later, remote work started and she also joined the job. I am also working remotely At least used to talk once a week even before she got the job, But after joining the job she also got busy and she was at home so I took the back step to give a call to her.

But the series of messages between us continued the same, she used to reply to my status and I used to comment on her post in that way we were in touch frequently. After that the corona effect reduced little by little and everyone started going to the office. Her base location is Hyderabad and my base location is Bangalore so there is no chance to meet at all.

But many times I thought that it would be good if she also came to Bangalore. Three years have passed and whenever I remember, I used to text her and she used to call me when she was free, but if I called her, there were cases where two people talked continuously for 2 hours without knowing the actual time.

At the same time, both of us wanted to change jobs. I don't know whether it was luck or coincidence, but both of us attempted the interview for the same company and luckily we got selected. I thought I would get a chance to meet her again, but bad luck, she accepted an offer from another company.

But this time, God listened to my wish, her base location also came to Bangalore, I also changed my job, her office is on the way to me, I was flew knowing that she will come to Bangalore, I was so happy that I wanted to meet her on the first day anyway, and I am happy, finally, after three years, I met her again.

$$\text{❧❧❧}$$

6

Yes, I'm in love

Meanwhile, the cab came and stopped in front of my room, I opened my eyes, paid the cab driver and went to my room and sat on the sofa, still thinking about her, same feeling again.

How I felt when I met her last time three years back, It's the same feeling again.

Is it possible to get the same feeling when you see a girl again after not seeing her for three years.

In our family, we think about sisters, mother, father. It is natural because it is a blood relation, there is nothing surprising in that, but when a new person is introduced somewhere and does not have any knowledge about her family, does this feeling arise?

Yes, I'm getting that feeling If this feeling is the definition of love then I am in love with her .

But this confusion is very new and I like it. I closed my eyes on the sofa and fell asleep without realizing it. But this time after many days, I don't know why, when I closed my eyes and fell asleep. My heart felt very happy.

The next day, I started to go to the office but while going in the car, on the way, all my thoughts were about yesterday's things only. Her room, her office and the restaurant where we met are all on the way to my office and whenever I see them, I remember her thoughts. I still couldn't avoid seeing her, so I started looking for a room near her room in .

In a week I found a room near to her room. The room I saw is 200 meters away from the room where she is living. from that room, her room can be seen very directly, whenever she comes out, I can see her clearly.That's why I chose the same room without any thought.

What's surprising here is that she doesn't know that I am always near her, every time she goes to her office, every time she walks after dinner, every time she does morning walk, every time I'm there to follow her. I used to follow her every time she went out , but anytime I couldn't dare to go in front of her. And we used to call and talk once a week for sure, she always called me after dinner and I was talking to her by following but she couldn't identify that.

ppp

7

Happy married life

18th June,2023 its evening, I completed my work and waiting for her in the balcony, 2 hours passes she didn't came.

I'm still waiting , after half an hour she came. It's actually late than usual.

By the time she comes she is talking on the phone. at least she didn't come for dinner either. Then I thought that I could meet her during the night walk and went for dinner.

While taking the dinner got a message

'Hay CK'

'Hay Amrutha'

'How are you CK'

'Ha I'm good Amrutha, how about you ?'

'I'm too good CK'

'what Amrutha ji, why the sudden message?'

'Nothing CK just remembering something' I was feeling very happy inside by seeing this kind of conversation with her and I continued.

'Do you Need any help?'

'feel free to ask me, I will never mind' I asked pericularly by sensing something needful

'Nothing CK, just casual'

After a minute again got the message from her

'*CK, shall we catch up for lunch tomorrow?*'

Every time I used to invite her , but this time I'm surprised she is inviting me to lunch. then I said

'*Sure, I would love to*'

'*OK bye CK,see you tomorrow*'

'*Bye, Good night*' Both stopped the conversation.

She didn't come for a night walk either, so I felt something strange was going on and slept on the sofa itself in the balcony.

᙭᙭᙭

Everything is in a rush in the house, relatives have already arrived, mom and dad are all dressed up and ready for some wedding, my college friends and colleagues have also arrived.

A wedding canopy has also been placed in front of our house. I am also ready with my wedding clothes.

My face lights up with happiness. All the relatives are laughing and talking together.

Just then I left with my parents in the car decorated for the wedding . Friends and relatives took the bus that they had already booked to the wedding hall.

After a one hour drive we reached the wedding hall. Before we arrived, the whole wedding hall became very noisy with the rest of the relatives. Seeing our car, friends and close relatives came and took me and made me sit on the wedding pews.

Everyone was laughing and talking, Panthulu garu was reading mantras, while my sister came from behind and said '*look at my sister- in -law is coming*'.

On the opposite side, a girl in wedding clothes is very well decorated and walking like an angel.

So before I raised my head and saw her face, my phone rang and the time was 5:30.

When I wake up, it's all a dream. I thought that this was the effect of last night, I thought that this kind of dream came because of thinking too much about her,

I woke up and got re fresh and went for morning workout.

The time is 10:30. I got a message with a ting sound, took out the phone and looked.

Hay CK

Hay Amrutha I replied

she asked *What time do you come?*

Let's meet whenever you can for your comfort. I will plan according to that.

Okey then same place @12

Perfect will see you @12

Yup see you there

But she doesn't know that I am close to her and that I am following her every day.

Ten minutes before 12 o'clock I went to the meeting place where we usually catch up, before going I took one with beautiful rose flowers for a bouquet . I did not understand why roses and lovers are near each other .What is the relationship between these things? But I can feel this once it comes to me.

Actually the main reason I came to the restaurant early was to give her a small surprise welcome, I took a single big rose bouquet. I thought I would present it to her and tell her about my love.I think it was a good moment to express my love, so I went to the restaurant where we used to meet and sat on the chair next to me and waited for her arrival.

She came exactly at 12 o'clock, even though I was watching her from the glass window next to me, she came inside the restaurant and looked back at the table where I was sitting.She was looking so beautiful to see wearing a white saree with free hair and she looked back at me and started walking towards me, while she was walking looks exactly like the goddess seen in last night's dream,

I stared at her without blinking. she came to me and talking like

'*Hay CK !! How are you?*'

Still I'm staring her

" *CK... What happened?*' she shoted with low

I picked up on her words

Sorry sorry..

Hay Amrutha. How are you?

Please come, have a seat.

'*When did you reach?*' she asked

'*10 minutes ago*' I said

'*So why do you want to meet? Anything to say?*' I came stright to point

she saisd '*Haa CK, one thing to say*'

I asked '*What is it?*'

'*I don't know if it's right or wrong.*' she continued explinaing then I asked with out patience

'*Aree tell the matter first*'

then she commanded '*Just, wait that's why I came right*'

'*Okey cool, take some water*'

Thank you

After a minute then I asked

'* tell me now*'

Yesterday my dad called and he said he had fixed a match for me and they asked me to go to my hometown.

I became silent for those words and she looked at me wondering what I would answer.

After a minute and a half I decided to break the silence and ask her to know what was on her mind.

What do you think? I asked

What could I say, I was scared to make this decision,

I don't understand now what to do.

Why are you scared, anyways you have a good job right then next is marriage. that's what you want right I said.

'*Do you love anyone?*' I asked

she said '*No , I don't know*'

After hearing this matter I don't understand what to do now.

'*That's why I wanted to meet you. If I could talk to you I would feel better.*'

'*Now I also don't have time , dad called me in the morning that he is coming, so i have to go to the bus stand to pick him up.*

But I have given promise to you, that's why I came now' she said.

Ever since I heard those words, I didn't know what to do, my face became dull. Then

I said, *let's uncle come, talk to him, explain to him, he will understand you.*

Yup, I hope so

Okey CK bye bye, I have to go she said and walking away And I didn't even try to stop her and she just went away.

Ever since she left I didn't know what to do. Many Questions came to mind like whether to tell her about my love or if she likes me or not? thinking like that, i remained silent.After about 15 minutes the waiter came and brought our favorite biryani.

Sometimes I used to scold my sister why she would skip meals.In general, if my sister is ever dull or someone scolds her , she will skip her meal then I used to scold her why would you skip your meal for someone. But now I am in the same situation.

Well, I started eating thinking that the food would be wasted, but the lump did not come down from my throat and my eyes got wet again without realizing it. It is not good for a boy to cry in public, so I took a parcel of food and went to my room, and I sat on the balcony and thought like this

Okey, don't feel

Let's tell her about my love

Yeah that's the only option I have now

Then I decided to talk to her tomorrow then I slept on the balcony thinking about it.

When I got up in the morning, it was 7:00, I looked at her room and she was still closing the door.

Okay, I thoughtthat I should call again in a little while and talk, but in the meantime, I ordered a big rose bouquet. Also, I got fresh up and I was making breakfast,

It was ten o'clock, so I called and connected the call to ask to meet.first time she did not pick up the call, tried again, this time she cut the call.

And The message was '*I went to my hometown ,right now I cannot talk.*'

When I saw that message, I couldn't handle the anger and pain all at once.Called her again an hour later.Still no response,two hours passed still no response, then I messaged 'call me when you are free'

The whole day passed, still no response nor call neither from her.I don't know what to do.So these two days passed, those two days I really saw hell. I used to look at her day by day and whenbut now she disappeared, I was feeling something unknown.

For those two days, when she was not walking at night, I felt something strange. I used to follow her on the whole road to her room, and all the memories of her were being remembered when she was not there.

After 2 days I got the message from her

'Hey CK , *Sorry yaar, I'm a little busy, that's why I'm late to reply.*'

I replied 'What's *wrong with you Is everything fine.?*'

'*I don't know But I have to tell you something. *' She is texting..

'*What is it?*' I replied

five minutes passed no response

One hour passed and there was no response.

I thought that she had gone to her hometown and was busy with some urgent work so might have forgotten.

ᛈᛈᛈ

8
With broken heart

That day it was night and I had completed my office work and was walking on the road where I used to walk.

While talking to mom and dad for a while, I got another call and it was Naveen.

Then I called Naveen after talking with my parents.

Hey bro

Hay Naveen , how are you?

Got the call after a long time, what's the matter?

Yeah bro, I'm good said Naveen

Where are you right now? Still in banglore? I got the question and answer both at a time.

Yes, bro

Okay, leave it. Do you know the matter? he asked

Matter!!, what ? I asked

The number next to you is getting married.

Sorry I don't understand I asked again

The girl next to your roll number is getting married tomorrow.

Ray, do you understand what you are talking about? I shouted on him

Rey, it's true. Sri has sent a message to the group.

After hearing that I was blank and mute.

Bro, you there ..

Ree....

You there......

After a minute he only hung up the call. After 10 minutes I came back to a normal situation and checked the message in the WhatsApp group where I found a wedding card and the marriage was tomorrow at 11:30.

Seeing it, I collapsed on the footpath right where I was.After seeing that my situation is like the force and pressure is more than when the volcano erupts.

Without thinking about anything else, I quickly went to my room, I went straight to the washroom, I sat on the top of the bathtub and shouted a lot. Unable to bear the pain, I was still crying and screaming.

Meanwhile, my school friend Badri came to my room to meet me. His office is near my room, he completed his work and came to my room. When he heard my crying, he came straight to my bedroom and saw that I was crying in the washroom.

He brought me outside and gave me some water and spoke to me soothingly.

He asked what happened, why are you crying like this? Then I told everything that happened and I also told about her marriage.

He heard what I said and said *ok let's go.*

Where will we go? I asked

He said, "*Let's go to marriage.*"

I said *no, it's not possible for me, I can't stand it after seeing her marriage.*

Listen to my words, let's go at least to see her for the last time as your love.

Then I said okay. He only packed up the luggage and started on the bike.

The time was already 11:00 PM, the first time that the bike journey at that time, the distance from Bangalore to Mysore is not big, so the maximum is 100 kilometers. I don't even have the patience to drive a bike, Badri himself drove a bike.

It was 3:00 AM at night. We saw the address from the wedding card and went directly to the function hall.

Badri said let's go inside.

I said no, it's already night, we will come early in the morning and meet.

Badri said, "*Okay, let's have some tea.*"

He didn't get any answer from me and he said ok and went to the tea shop next to the road.

Looking at the front, the whole function hall is very bright with lighting, then I felt this in my mind.

'*This is the last night of my love. It is the wedding of the girl I love. And I am outside the wedding function hall and there is no chance to talk to her. Please god even the enemy should not have trouble like me.*'

Badri came after drinking tea and we both took a room in the hotel. Bhadri said don't think about anything and sleep for a while and whatever will happen let's see in the morning. And he took his bed sheet and slept.

I don't have any feelings, I just lie in bed thinking that I can't do anything except pain.

It was 7:30 in the morning when I got up because we were tired from the bike journey. We Both got up and freshened up and at 10 o'clock we went straight from the hotel to the marriage function hall.

When I was going inside, my college friends were in the entrance. Everyone was sitting together and talking. As soon as they saw me, everyone came and took me with them. Even though I forced them to explain something but they did not listen, they were in their flow.

So they are talking about college matters, but my condition is something that I can't tell anyone. Meanwhile, someone said from the back, okay, let's talk to the bride once, she won't have time, she will be busy.

Everyone has started . Then I thought that this is what I needed and followed them to the bride room. Amrutha is still decorating. We all went to her room and all their relatives were there.I stayed behind without her sight , each of them went Individually and said their wishes.

In the end, I was the only one left. Finally in one end, I was standing in front of her, we both looked at each other. There were no words between us, only our eyes were talking, and half a minute passed. Then they went to pick her up from there saying that it would be time for Muhurta. As she was going, she turned and gave me a look that I will never forget in my life.

All the friends went and sat opposite the mandapam. Even now, the remaining two of the people of their three idiots gang are standing next to her, there is no reaction from her, she is not talking to anyone.

I did not want to stay there as soon as I saw it, I wiped my eyes and came out of the mandap. Bhadri and I both started on the bike and we didn't know where to go. We just took the bike and he was sitting behind me.I, who was already riding the bike, didn't know what to do, I didn't know where to go. who was going straight and fast on the highway, Bhadri also tried to stop me a couple of times, but there was no answer from me and he lost patience and stopped asking me.

Driving like that, we reached somewhere on the hill and it was already night. I was driving in such pain that I couldn't take it anymore, I stopped the bike, got off the bike and climbed the big rock and started screaming.

I'm wrong,
I'm sorry my love.
I always have to tell you about my love
I'm wrong,
I'm wrong,
I'm wrong,
I love you Amrutha, I love you so much,
I could have told you this way before , but i couldn't,
I'm sorry but I love you so much.

Seeing me screaming so loudly, Badri came to him and spoke soothingly. You should have told her about this sometime but you were late, what can we do? Don't worry, life gives us a second chance again.

But I did not listen to his words and sat there on the rock. Then he started searching where we are? It was somewhere on the ghat road in Coorg hill station.then he took a bike to drive and I sat behind him, he started the bike. We both went to a hotel and booked a room, and it was around 10 in the night , he went and brought some outside food. Both started eating but. I couldn't, he was observing everything and he was calm as if he knew how painful it is.

Who Are You?

I woke up the next morning . Time is around 10 in the morning and I'm alone in the room,

I started getting up and took steps towards the balcony. Meanwhile I started calling Bhadri, he told me that he went outside to do some work.

There was a beautiful view from the balcony. There was a green theme painted by nature around the valleys and fog falling like a rain in every place and the sun was looking like a playing hide and seek along with the clouds.

But all of this beautiful nature didn't satisfy me, still I'm in yesterday's pain. Then suddenly my phone started ringing .it was from home I started talking with them.

After a while they hung up the phone. After that I threw it on the teapot and started looking at nature in front of me by thinking about something.

Again my phone rang, this time it was an Unknown number. I don't have good mood to talk so i ignored it.

Again it started ringing, this time also it's same number. Then I answered the call

"Hello, who is this?" I asked

"Is it talking to Chandra?" asked a lady voice

"Yes,it's me. Please go head" I said

"I love you!!!"

my reaction was like *"What !!!!!!!!!!!!!"*

www.ingramcontent.com/pod-product-compliance
Lightning Source LLC
Chambersburg PA
CBHW020939160726
47993CB00007B/2846